THE VAMPIRE'S LAIR

A PARANORMAL ROMANCE

AJ TIPTON

Copyright © 2017 by AJ Tipton

All rights reserved.

No part of this book may be reproduced in any form or by any electronic or mechanical means, including information storage and retrieval systems, without written permission from the author, except for the use of brief quotations in a book review.

This book is for sale to adult audiences only. It contains substantial sexually explicit scenes and graphic language which may be considered offensive by some readers. All sexually active characters in this work are 18 years of age or older.

This is a work of fiction. All characters, names, places and incidents appearing in this work are fictitious. Any resemblance to real persons, living or dead, organizations, events or locales is purely coincidental.

Cover art photos provided by BigStock.com, Morgue Files, Flickr.com, and Upsplash.com. Graphic design by CirceCorp

"You chicken?" Danny called out across the bar. *What am I getting myself into?* The eight-foot tall troll lumbered up to Danny's table and Danny sipped at his glass of O positive blood, focusing on looking casual even as his stomach churned.

The troll bristled, the rocks protruding from his skull standing at their peak.

"What did you say to me?" With each word came a punctuation of spit, sending chunks of saliva and what looked like tree bark splattering across the surface of Danny's table.

Trolls were huge creatures, rarely under seven-feet tall, but this one was well over nine, his head dusting the roof of the bar. Blagfor had an impressive biome of lichen running along his left side, starting at his shoulders and traveling down to his waist, and looked like he'd been chiseled off the side of a mountain.

Danny flexed his hands, steeling his nerves. *You've gone up against worse than this*, he reminded himself. As an investigator for the vampire king, and a vampire prince himself, he had taken down vampire crime lords, wrestled the vampire kingdom away from an evil tyrant, and once even stole the last fry off of his sire's plate. But somehow, none of those felt quite as perilous as the walking mountain staring down at him.

"I *said*..." Danny downed the rest of his drink in a single gulp and banged the glass down for emphasis. "Wanna arm wrestle?"

All eyes turned toward them and, for a long moment, everything was silent. AUDREY'S bar wasn't much to look at: a tall, wooden shack in the middle of nowhere with beaten up furniture and no ambiance to speak of, but it was *the* spot for supernaturals. Tonight it was stuffed to the brim with pixies, yetis, witches, werewolves, and some folks with spikes Danny couldn't even identify. All of them drooled in their excitement to see a drunk, rich clown get taken down by a troll.

Which was precisely the idea.

"Do you really think you can take *me* down, little man?" The troll sneered with what few teeth he had left. "I am Blagfor the mighty!" His posse of trolls all roared in support, shaking the rafters.

"I know I can. In fact..." Danny pulled a stack of hundred-dollar bills from the interior pocket of his leather jacket and slapped them down on the table. "I'll bet on it." Danny let the muscles in his face sag, swaying in his seat for effect.

Dumb, drunk, and rich. Danny repeated the mantra in his head. *I need them to believe I'm dumb, drunk, and rich.* He never considered himself much of an actor, but the investigation hinged on him calling on his inner trust-fund brat to put on a good show.

Blagfor opened his arms and called out to his friends. "This'll be the easiest money I ever made." He cracked his knuckles and shook, his joints all snapping at once in a horrible chorus.

Danny placed his elbow down onto the table and slipped for good measure, nearly smacking his face on the table before catching himself at the last moment with his free hand and righting himself. The trolls laughed and slapped each other on their backs, their focus never leaving the pile of cash.

Blagfor planted his elbow across from Danny's and took his hand. Danny stifled a laugh at how surprisingly soft the troll's palm was.

"Three," Blagfor said.

"Two." Danny's hand closed tightly around Blagfor's palm in a crushing grip.

"One!" They shouted in unison, both pushing against each other with all their might.

Blagfor's right side bulged, the muscles in his rock-hard arms straining for dominance.

But he didn't know Danny was a vampire.

To the trolls, Danny appeared as a tall, Asian human in his twenties, fit but not muscular. It made it easy to miss that it wasn't a fair fight.

Danny feigned a struggle, his vampire strength keeping Blagfor's hand dangerously close to the surface of the table. *Stick to the plan*, Danny chastised himself. Slowly, Danny allowed his arm to be pushed backwards by the troll's strength, pressing just enough to show he wasn't giving the game away. He bit back a sigh of relief as his fist smashed down under Blagfor's. The slam echoed through the bar, overpowered by the cheer ringing out from the spectating patrons.

Small flashes of light came from the raised cell phones all around him. *Perfect,* Danny thought, hiding a triumphant smile. Social media was a blessing in so many ways for the intrepid private investigator.

Blagfor let out a roar, raising his arms to the ceiling and painting the bar with his impressive stench. More cameras flashed.

Danny, closest to the troll's armpits, stifled a gag as he slid over the stack of cash. He made sure to smile gamely. "Not too bad, troll."

Blagfor leaned in to whisper, "You almost had me there, vampire. Maybe next time you'll give me a *real* match."

"Next time," Danny said with a wink. Blagfor smiled, pocketed the cash, and lumbered back to his friends.

Time to take this up a notch.

Danny jumped on top of his barstool, balancing easily on the shaky wood. "Never let it be said that Prince Danny Dal is a poor loser. The next round is on me!" He pointed over to the bartender, whose long black braids were hypnotically floating above her head in a rhythmic dance. "Make sure to give 'em the good stuff, Lola!"

Further bursts of photos flashed in Danny's direction and the suddenly infamous vampire prince hopped to the ground. Bear and dragon shifters slapped him on the back, a couple witches gave him thumbs up, as the crowd surged toward the bar for their round.

Drinks flowed, Blagfor bought a round, loudly proclaiming it was with Danny's money, and Danny checked his watch for the second time that hour. *I couldn't be making more of a scene if I wanted to. Where are they?*

If they didn't show up soon, he feared he was going to have to start up the karaoke machine. Usually his private eye gigs resulted in him chasing around adulterers and embezzlers. But this time was different. His sire, the Vampire King Christopher Dal, had sent him to investigate rumors of abuse at a vampire pleasure palace, the Blood Oasis. The rumors were little more than gossip, and Danny wasn't expecting to find anything, but it still felt good to be on an official mission for the palace.

But *finding* the place to investigate was tricky. The Blood Oasis's location was secret and invite-only. Danny tried not to fidget in his seat. Surely, the club had somebody on their payroll scoping out social media for easy marks?

"I've got a thousand bucks for whoever can beat me at

darts!" He called out to the room, grabbing a pile of them off the board next to him.

Warm fingers closed around Danny's hand, encapsulating the dart.

"Throwing sharp objects in your state is probably not the best idea." The woman's voice came from behind him. "Especially with so many people taking video."

The human female's scent hit him like all the hidden notes of a complex wine coming together at once. It wasn't just her skin--the sweetness of vanilla with an underlying deep scent of earth and moss--but her emotions singing to him from her blood. Smelling the emotions of non-vampires was one of his favorite advantages of being a vampire, although sometimes the insights were less than flattering. She was excited and scared, but mostly annoyed. *At me, probably,* Danny thought. Knowing he was being a jackass on purpose didn't make her frustration any more enjoyable.

She was stunning: a tall brunette with pale skin and brown eyes flecked with gold. Just looking at her, Danny felt like he'd missed a step in the dark and gotten the breath knocked out of him. He froze, grasping for his mask of indifferent rich boy that kept slipping under her penetrating gaze.

"Prince Dal?" The woman released his hand from her grip, placing the captive dart back onto the pub table. "My name is Robin Ballard. There's something I'd like to discuss with you." She guided him to a secluded table in the back of the bar, away from the ruckus of the crowd.

Danny resisted the urge to pull away from her, to go back to his plan of conspicuous money-losing. But there was something about her that intrigued him. *The Blood Oasis needs time to marshal their contacts anyway,* he told himself.

He glanced around and there was no one in earshot. "Ms.

Ballard," he said, dropping his drunken act. "I only have a few moments to spare. How can I help you?" She sat straight in her chair, her poise and the cut of her black suit all business. Danny pressed down his disappointment. She likely had a case to report to the vampire king. Since Danny's sire was crowned king, Christopher's sirelings had been busy uncovering the scandals which the former king hadn't bothered to police.

A blood cocktail slid into place beside his elbow and Danny nodded thanks to the bartender, Lola, as she also placed a whiskey on the rocks next to Robin. The beautiful woman thanked Lola before turning her gold-flecked gaze back onto Danny's face. Anxiety churned in Robin's blood. He fought the instinct to lay a reassuring hand on her arm.

"I appreciate your time. Feel free to call me Robin." She sipped at her drink and smiled. "I *thought* that drunk act you were pulling out there was a bit on the nose. I'm glad to see you can handle your blood." She splayed her fingers out onto the table. "Since you're in a rush, I'll be blunt. I need you to turn me into a vampire."

What? Danny resisted the urge to laugh incredulously. "I appreciate your gumption. But, to be equally blunt, no." He moved to stand. Danny had decided a long time ago he was done with siring.

Robin placed her hand over his, freezing him in place. "It does sound ridiculous, I agree. Please sit, there's a lot of information you don't have."

Danny raised an eyebrow, but took his seat. As she spoke, Danny sniffed out a scent he hated to pick up from her: fear.

"I can't say I'm not curious." He took a generous swig of his drink. "You have until I'm done with this cocktail."

Robin's words tumbled out, chasing each other in her

haste to explain. "I'm a conservationist, working to protect the endangered Scarred Vultrich. It's a fascinating bird, but isn't very attractive." She chuckled. "It basically looks like an ostrich and a vulture got smashed together. It's also nocturnal, which makes it even harder for people to sympathize with. There's not a lot of support to save animals that aren't cute."

"I imagine there isn't." Danny didn't know much about wildlife and tried not to smirk at his hideous mental approximation of what the vultrich might look like.

"These birds can breed and thrive in a very small habitat. Today, I lost a fight to a developer that would pave over *half* of what's left. I need to be able to defend these incredible creatures. I need the *time* to make sure they're safe." She pounded a fist down onto the table, shaking the glassware.

"So you figured you'd just swing down to the local pub and grab yourself some immortality?" Danny leaned back in his chair. "How would a human like you even know how to find a vampire?"

"My college roommate, Samantha, is a witch. She comes from a big family of witches, and I spend my holidays with them." Sadness washed the air around her and Danny fought to keep his expression casual. Centuries living among short-lived humans had taught him a thing or two about mourning. The woman was hurting, and the pain of it had driven her here.

Robin smiled and Danny's heart cracked a little. To smile through her grief like that, it took an admirable amount of strength.

"Samantha's aunts' gossip told me more about the supernatural world than I could have discovered from years of research."

"There's a lot more to being a vampire than you could possibly understand just from idle chit-chat." Danny looked down into the thick, red liquid in his glass.

"I know some vampires turn their sirelings and then never see them again. This barely has to inconvenience you at all." Robin placed her hand over Danny's. Her touch sent fissions of lightning along his skin and he shivered. *Who is this woman?* Her expression was grave. "I've been thinking about this for a very long time and I did my research."

How can some birds be so important? Danny's curiosity threatened to get the better of him. "No." He downed his glass in a single gulp. "Siring a new vampire is a tremendous responsibility, and it's not one I take lightly anymore." Burned once, he didn't need that again. "You'll have to find somebody else to help you on your quest." He stood, throwing some cash on the table. "The drinks are on me."

Robin's face turned bright red. "You *selfish* sonofa..." She screamed, but he hurried out of earshot. Walking away from her felt like pulling against a riptide.

"Prince Dal, your majesty." A sleek gentleman in a pinstripe suit stepped in Danny's path, giving a small bow. "I heard you were...entertaining yourself here."

A quick whiff revealed the man as a cheetah shifter. Danny couldn't smell the man's emotions, though, a clear sign the messenger was also a vampire. Shifters rarely decided to become vampires, but immortality could be tempting to all types. He handed Danny a silver card, with the words "Blood Oasis" embossed in a deep red on the front.

Danny resisted the urge to sigh in relief. The Blood Oasis must have sent their fastest employee once they heard of Danny's whereabouts. He could stop acting like a drunken fool and finally get to work.

The cheetah shifter raised an eyebrow at Danny, leering a little. "If you are seeking a more *stimulating* environment, I would like to extend an invitation to the Blood Oasis. It's a vampiric pleasure palace beyond your wildest dreams, and only available to an *exclusive* clientele." He flipped the card over, his thumbprint pressing a rune imbedded in the paper. Small lights on the card flared to life. "This card is spelled to lead you to the Oasis."

Danny turned the card over in his hand. The address flashed along the back of the heavy card stock, followed by an arrow pointing in the direction of the Blood Oasis.

"That sounds delightful. I'll be sure to stop by," Danny said.

The cheetah shifter bowed and spotted fur rippled in a wave over his skin, enveloping him as his form shrunk and transformed before Danny's eyes until a large cat with a long, swishing tail stood in a pool of pinstripe suit. The cat carefully folded the clothes away and darted out of the bar.

Danny glanced over at the corner where Robin had been fuming, but she was gone. *It's for the best*, he told himself, not quite believing it.

THE BLOOD OASIS business card twisted and twirled on his dashboard as he drove deeper into the woods, the paper lighting up with arrows and instructions that would probably have been more impressive if Danny didn't recognize a simple GPS spell knock-off.

As he drove, Danny kept catching a glimpse of a dented, red sedan in his rear view mirror. *Was the club keeping tabs on him?* A shiver of unease rippled through him. *Perhaps there is something to these rumors.* He cut his lights, turned off to the side of the road, letting the red sedan fly past him so he could get a better look at the driver.

Robin.

He chuckled. *Nice try.* The woman really was determined to find a vampire sire. Even with his own past disappointments with sireing, he might be tempted to help find her a suitable sire. But the mission called.

The Blood Oasis card chirped at him, the spell frustrated he had gone off route. He backed out and sped away. Behind him, the road was clear.

ROBIN'S HANDS tightened around her steering wheel as she watched Danny Dal's brake lights disappear around a corner. She figured he must still be headed in the direction of the Blood Oasis.

Excellent. She'd managed to get a quick glance at the Blood Oasis card back at AUDREY'S, and had jotted down the address. It was lucky, since she'd never been great at following people. The one time she'd tried to track down a construction foreman to show him pictures of baby vultrich, she'd gotten the cops called on her. Looking at Danny's final destination, she took the long way around to avoid having to be stealthy. Danny would have to reconsider turning her once he realized she wasn't going to leave him in peace until she got what she needed.

Robin followed her GPS out of the city and up into the hills, the road narrowing from four lanes, to two, down to one narrow strip of asphalt with trees clustered close on either side. The moonlight transformed the trees' bare branches into skeletal arms reaching across the road toward one another, ready to join forces to submerge the road entirely. When the road curved around a cliff, the lights from the city below were laid out like a kid's toy, but the slim crescent of moon did little to illuminate anything beyond her car's beams.

Her phone buzzed, a picture of her college roommate, Samantha, giving the finger to the camera popping up across the screen. Robin clicked it onto speaker, keeping her eyes on the road.

"Hey Samantha, I'm--"

Samantha cut her off. "I know exactly what you're doing, and you need to cut this shit out."

"You don't understand." Robin concentrated on sounding logical. Earlier that day, she'd driven by the construction site. Broken eggshells lay caught in the spokes of a tractor's bucket, fragments of baby birds mashed up among the rocks and dirt. Vultrich slept during the day, so Robin hadn't expected to see any, but she could have sworn she heard one's little squawks of distress. So many dead, all because she hadn't gotten there soon enough, hadn't done enough. Her jaw tightened.

"I'm the only one who cares enough about these birds to keep them safe. And if becoming a blood-guzzling immortal is what I need to do, then--"

"It isn't worth it," Samantha said. "Do you really want to never age, never have kids, and be *totally* beholden to your sire's will? Because that's what their *hortari* sire compulsion is, sweetie. You will *have* to do everything your sire says. You didn't like following instructions to build that bookshelf because you thought the directions were too constricting. How the hell are you going to feel when your sire tells you to smile because it makes you look pretty, and your lips move against your will? Are your birds worth that?"

Robin didn't hesitate. "Yes."

Somewhere out there, the vultrich were beginning to wake up. Did they already know half of their nesting ground was demolished? Would their screams when they found their broken nests be loud enough for neighboring businesses to hear what they'd done?

"Danny Dal isn't the responsible type," Robin continued. "He'll just sire me and then let me go do what I want, as long as I'm out of his hair. Everything he's done tonight makes him a perfect sire: wealthy, irresponsible, and a little stupid." *And ridiculously hot,* she didn't say.

When the bartender, Lola, first pointed him out at AUDREY'S, Robin's breath had burst out of her body and her nipples immediately tightened in the most extreme reaction of horniness she'd ever experienced. It was a good thing he was cocky and dumb. Having a clever sire would ruin her plans. She couldn't get distracted from her mission.

Samantha sighed. "Just tell me that you're going to be smart about this. Spend some time with him, make sure that your impression from watching him for a few hours is enough to make a decision that will impact you *for eternity*."

A mansion loomed on top of the next hill. The Blood Oasis's sign was small, barely a plaque set inside a stone column next to a long driveway that curved off into the dark woods.

"Samantha, I have to go. I just arrived."

"Where?" Her voice dripped with suspicion.

"At home." Parked cars lined the edge of the drive and she pulled into an open spot. Robin opened her door and a gust of cold air stabbed at her bare legs and arms. Looking down, she was grateful she'd packed a spare outfit in addition to the suit she'd worn at the bar.

"You're a bad liar." Samantha sighed. "You're going to a vampire bar, aren't you? Those are basically brothels, Robin. That is so not your scene. Please, tell me you're not still doing this."

"I have to. Goodbye, Sam."

"Wait! Tell me where you are and I'll come get you. Robin-_"

Robin hung up the phone, and then turned it off before Samantha could barrage her with more calls.

Yesterday, she'd been so sure she was going to be able to halt construction of that damn mini-mall. The local wildlife offices were on her side and were ready to come out and conduct inspections. She'd reached out to the U.S. Fish and Wildlife Service for assistance in enforcing the Endangered Species Act, and to the U.S. Army Corps of Engineers about classifying the nesting grounds as protected wetlands. She'd sent cease and desist letters to the construction company, and written over a hundred letters to her local Congressman to help advocate for the protection of an endangered species in his district. She'd finally gotten a member of his staff on the phone, and they'd seemed open to putting out a press release calling for the protection of their unique wildlife.

But all the construction company had to do was roll their tractors a week earlier than planned and it was all over. They would pay a fine that would barely put a dent in their overall profits, and they were busy publishing statements congratulating themselves on "cleaning out the disease-carrying vermin infesting the area."

Robin held her purse close to her chest and concentrated

on not wobbling on the uneven cobblestone walkway up to the Blood Oasis.

Her steps slowed as she neared. It looked like a state mansion from a Jane Austen novel, at least six stories tall of white stone, with graceful, Grecian columns, and two curving stone staircases winding up to a fifteen-foot arched doorway. Pulsing colored lights and pumping bass music blared from the first floor, while the upper floor windows lay quiet.

If Samantha was right and this place was a brothel, then having a private upstairs for guests to enjoy themselves made sense. Her pulse quickened.

Perhaps Danny will want to have some fun before he turns me?

She shook off the thought before the fantasy of Danny's hands teasing her breasts and his mouth pressing against her neck became too vivid.

She wasn't here for *that*.

Robin was here to become a vampire.

Get strength to break their tractors before they can destroy nests.

Get *time* to build advocacy and teach others to appreciate the vultrich's rare beauty and wonder.

Danny Dal was just a means to an end.

A slot in the front door slid open and a pair of steely eyes looked over her outfit, which was less a dress and more a small piece of fabric wound around her. Her favorite part was the pink banded choker drawing attention to the long line of her neck and pulled-up brunette locks. Blood Oasis might be officially "invite only," but Robin had been to enough clubs in college to know that sometimes skin was its own all-access pass.

The enormous bouncer in a black suit held the door open wide.

"Welcome to the Blood Oasis. Let us cater to your fantasies." His voice was deep and musical, but the words were flat like he was reading them off cue cards.

Working the door at a vampire bar can't be the most glamorous job, Robin guessed. *All the fun happens inside.* She smiled at him in thanks and he gave her a stiff nod in reply before closing the door and sliding in the lock with a loud click.

Robin shivered.

Just find Danny. Considering the out-of-the-way route she took to get here, he had to have arrived before her. Looking around, she couldn't help but notice the interior was as gorgeous as the exterior. The foyer opened up into entrances for two different rooms: the one off to the right looked like an intimate library with dark-paneled wood, low light, walls covered in rows of book spines, and the sound of a live jazz band playing. Something about the cloistered, safe space made her think of the vultrich sanctuaries she visited at night with her parents.

The room to the left was wide open with glass windows covering the wall looking out into the swaying trees. Fun dance music and flashing colored lights filled the space while waiters circled with colorful cocktails filled to the brim. It was exactly the kind of place she'd spent too much time in during her college years, the lights and sounds making her wish she'd thought to pack her old goth clubbing gear. *Whatever happened to my knee-high boots? They'd be perfect for this place.*

Everywhere, pairs and trios danced and talked, black leather and flesh pressed against one another, makeup thick and smeared, hands roaming. Hormones and lust saturated the air. Blood flooded Robin's cheeks, wetness pooling between her legs as she looked around.

In the darkened library to the right, on a low couch, a man's head was buried deep between a woman's spread legs, her fingers clutching at his hair, and her head thrown back into an open-mouthed, silent scream of pleasure. A staff member caught the woman's eye, handed her a key, and pointed toward the stairs. The woman nodded, grabbed the kneeling man's hand, and the two ran towards the rooms upstairs.

I think I love this place, Robin thought.

Over in the dance room, a pair of men wearing skin-tight leather chaps and nothing else grinded a scantily-clad woman between them, one kissing her neck while the other's hands roamed over her shirt and down to caress her thighs. Two other men were heartedly making out against the window, their hips thrusting fast in time to the music as their hands wandered under each other's shirts. Robin felt surrounded by life and sex and fun. If this was the vampire lifestyle Samantha was so worried about, Robin was *in*.

Robin found the bar in the back of the dance room and ordered a cranberry juice so it would look like she was drinking a cocktail while still keeping her head clear. At some point, she wanted to come back and enjoy this place properly, but tonight she was going to find a sire.

"Hello, beautiful." The man's voice to her right was kind, but with the same flatness as the bouncer at the door. "I just *had* to come talk to you. Sweetness is my weakness."

Her eyes widened. The man was *definitely* a vampire. His canines were so elongated, they poked out to dig into his lower lip. He was taller than her by at least a foot and well-built, but his posture was slumped and his arms wrapped around himself in a protective gesture that made him look small and vulnerable. He wore jeans and a white shirt unbuttoned nearly to his navel so it flapped open, showing rows of hard muscles. The effect was supposed to be sexy, but mostly she just thought he looked cold.

"Are you okay?" she asked.

He straightened, his eyes darting around the room. "Of course!" Something about his voice was too jolly, forced. "I'm just so happy to be talking with the sexiest woman here. I mean, just look at you. Roses are red, violets are blue, but I didn't know perfect until I met you." He sounded like he was miserable about every word.

"What's your name?" she asked, hoping some friendliness would help ease the sadness in his shoulders. "Do you come here often?"

"I'm Seyah." He smiled, the edges pinched. "I'm here every night." He glanced upward and Robin spotted a camera's eye blinking red from the corner of the ceiling.

"You work here?" she whispered. When he nodded, still smiling the non-smile, she asked, "Are you okay?"

Seyah stepped away from her. "You know, I can see you're not really into this. You have a lovely evening. I know you'll find someone here who will cater to your fantasies." He disappeared into the throng of dancers.

Robin considered going after him, but he was obviously scared of something. She glanced around the room again, feeling unsettled. The music felt too loud now. The flashing lights made her head pound. The movements of some of the dancers looked too jerky, like marionettes being pulled around on strings, with their expression hard masks as their partners danced on top of them. Cradling her juice, Robin made her way around the outside of the room.

Just find Danny, and get out of here.

Could he have already found someone and gone upstairs? The thought made her even more uncomfortable.

The darkened library was quiet with the band on break sipping drinks in the corner. Fewer people milled around the dim space, most of the pairs gone. Robin assumed they had gone to dance, or upstairs to complete their evening. One woman lay draped across the back of a padded sofa playing with the long, red hair of a large man sitting near her. She was smiling and giggling at something he was saying, but she flinched when he touched her hand.

Maybe Samantha was right. I made a mistake coming here.

A petite, blond woman chatting with the musicians burst into a twinkling bell-like laughter so loud it filled the room. The sound was so happy, so purely joyous, Robin felt herself drawn toward the small woman like a magnet. She wore more clothes than most of the other women there combined, although the tightness of the red dress hugging her curves left nothing to the imagination. When she caught Robin looking her, the woman smiled and beckoned Robin forward.

"Hi there, you look a little lost." The woman's voice was as light and pretty as her laugh.

"I guess I am," Robin said. She searched the woman's features for any of Seyah's flatness or flinching, but the woman's bright smile lit up her eyes like twin glowing lamps. "I came here looking for someone, but I haven't seen him around."

"Stood up on a date? I'm so sorry, honey." She rested a hand lightly on Robin's arm. "You know the best way to get over a guy? Get under a new one." She laughed and pointed to a couple of the musicians who were sizing up Robin like she was a steak.

Robin stepped back hurriedly. "No, that's not it." *Although if Danny looked at me that way, I wouldn't be saying no*. The thought flashed by too fast for her to clamp it down. Robin continued on, talking quickly. "I'm actually looking for a vampire."

The woman smiled and Robin noticed for the first time how long her canines dipped in her mouth.

"Well, you found one." She held out a hand. "My name is Nia Ashmore."

Robin shook Nia's hand, appreciating the brisk strength in the woman's grip. "Robin Ballard. It's nice to meet you."

"Have you seen the gardens? They're not as stunning at night as I'm told they are during the day, but they're still lovely."

"Fresh air sounds amazing. Thanks."

Nia's stunning smile flashed again and Robin felt herself relaxing into the woman's company. They chatted easily as they walked through the mansion about music, the last movie they saw in theaters, where they went to college, and bad dates they'd been on recently. By the time they made it outside, Robin knew she'd found an amazing new friend. Nia was articulate, funny, and kind, with a positive viewpoint Robin knew to be all too rare.

"I'm so glad I came tonight," Robin said, wrapping an arm around Nia's diminutive shoulders.

"Me too." Nia smiled. She brushed her fingers along the back of Robin's hand. "I think you're exactly the kind of friend I've been looking for."

The gardens were just as stunning as Nia claimed: a landscaped vista of crisscrossing rocky streams, with a gazebo and roses that curled into each other in rich, romantic bouquets.

Robin smiled, settling down on one of the stone benches that looked out onto the gardens.

"This is beautiful. You know, this place would be a great nesting place for vultrich." Robin sighed and leaned back against the bench. "With all these rocks and little nooks, it would be perfect."

"Vultrich? Those nocturnal vulture-looking birds that live around here?"

"Yes!" Robin grabbed Nia's hands and pulled her into a tight hug. "Nobody ever seems to know them, and they're amazing."

"Really?" Nia studied Robin's face. "I wouldn't have ever guessed I'd see someone so worked up over vultrich." She smiled, tilting her head to the side. "But then, I spent six months after college living in the rainforest helping save tropical frogs, so I know what it's like to feel passionately about a creature nobody else seems to care about."

"You worked with tropical frogs? That's so great!" Robin wanted to never stop hugging Nia, this extraordinary woman who seemed to understand every part of her completely. "Protecting the vultrich is my life's work. It's why I came here tonight, why I wanted to find a vampire."

"Oh?" Nia's smile was as curious as a kitten.

"Yes, I was looking to be turned into a vampire so that I can have a fighting chance of saving their habitat. I need time to convince others to love them as much as I do."

"Well, *I* could turn you," Nia said slowly. She smiled at Robin. "In fact, I would love to be your sire. I always have a good instinct about people, and I knew I would like you from the second we met. I have a vast family of vampires I've turned, and I've never regretted any for a moment."

Could it be that easy? Robin's heart started to beat fast. "You'd really turn me? Tonight?"

"Why not? There's no reason to delay." Nia stood up and held out her hand to Robin. "I can set everything up for the ritual upstairs right now."

Robin took Nia's hand and got to her feet.

"There's a ritual?" Samantha had never mentioned a ritual, but Robin supposed even witches wouldn't know every detail about how vampires were turned. She followed Nia back into the house, turning right and going up a flight of stairs so narrow and unadorned Robin doubted they were usually used by guests.

"Of course we have a ritual! We're not savages," Nia said over her shoulder as she pulled Robin up the stairs. "Welcoming a new vampire to eternity is a big deal, we want to make sure it has the proper amount of ceremony."

Nia's grip on Robin's hand was tight and confident as she led her down a long corridor lined with numbered doors like at a hotel. Groaning, screams of "yes! more!" and the sound of slapping flesh coming from the doorways left Robin with no suspicion about what was happening on this floor. She blushed, feeling arousal pooling again in her lower stomach.

Would I recognize Danny's voice if I heard it? She wondered, but pushed the thought away. She didn't need Danny anymore. She had Nia: lovely, environmentally-active Nia who saved tree frogs and loved comic book movies.

Nia opened the last door on the hallway, this one marked "Private" and held it open for Robin to step through.

Robin paused.

When did Nia set all this up?

The entire room was lit with candles that surrounded the room on all sides, drawing attention to a huge, golden altar that took up one of the walls. Two hooded figures stood on either side of the altar, their robes blood red, and their hands clasped in front of them. Robin guessed they were men from the breadth of their shoulders, but it was hard to tell. On the altar were only two items: a silver knife with ornate filigree on the handle, and a chalice larger than Robin's head.

"This is---" Robin couldn't find the right word. *Ridiculous? Cheesy? Over-the-top? B-movie level dramatic?* "All for the ritual?"

Nia pulled her into the room and led her to a small pillow at the base of the altar. "Kneel here."

Nia whispered something to the hooded men and the three of them huddled together around the knife and the cup. They chanted together softly, their words indistinguishable.

Holy shit, this is actually happening.

"What about the *hortari*? We never even talked about that," Robin said. "Do you, um, force the vampires you sire to do things?"

Nia turned, holding the chalice. It was now filled an inch-deep with thick, red blood. "I'm your friend, Robin. I would never make you do anything you didn't want to do." She took Robin's hands and wrapped them around the cup, pushing the lip toward Robin's mouth.

Everything's happening so fast.

"Now, drink this before it gets cold," Nia instructed. "Be the protector your birds deserve."

Yes. I will be their protector. Robin brought the cup to her lips and took a long gulp of the blood. It tasted like tap water run through rusty pipes, with a thick texture like cream that choked her all the way down.

"Was that it?" Robin asked. Her head felt she was floating,

or uncomfortably high. She tried to raise a hand to wipe a bead of sweat off of her forehead and her arm felt so heavy, she could barely lift it. The room wobbled in front of her, everything going off kilter.

"Yeah, it's done, sweet cheeks," said a rough voice from the figure on the right.

Through a haze, she saw the two robed men shake off their hoods. Even with very different features, they had the same hard expressions, the same cruel glints in their eyes. The one on the right who had spoken had a long scar down his cheek, which carved his lips into a grimace.

"Who are you?" Robin's mouth felt like it was stuffed with cotton, her thoughts churning at a slow chug.

Nia ignored her, nodding to the one with the scarred face. "Seth, test her." Her voice was unrecognizable now. It had dropped an octave, each word clipped and sharp.

Something is very wrong. Fear bit like frozen spikes into Robin's chest. She tried to rise to her feet, every muscle feeling like it weighed fifty pounds.

"Sit down," Seth said.

Every muscle demanded that Robin sit down. Her body froze. Her knees bent and then gave out, sending her spilling to the floor. She fought against it, trying to stand, but it was no use. Her body was no longer under her command.

"Now, slap yourself across the face." Seth chuckled.

Robin watched with horror as her own hand rose against her command, drew back, and hit her hard across the face. She screamed out in pain and surprise.

"What's happening?" Robin yelled. She looked back and forth between Nia and Seth. *Nia* was supposed to be the only one whose sire command could compel her to do anything.

Seth pulled back the sleeve of his robe, revealing a long cut down his forearm. "You're mine, bitch."

"No!" Robin yelled, fighting to get to her feet.

"Sit down and stay there until I say so," Seth said.

Robin collapsed back onto the floor, her legs locked into a seated position. She tried to grab at her foot to pull it up using her hands, but it felt like it was welded to the floor.

Oh my god. This isn't happening. This isn't happening. The room was still hazy. *What have I done?*

Robin stared at Nia. "Why?"

Nia's angelic face now twisted into a sneer. "I'm not about to waste my time on every fool human that walks in this place. I have a few choice sirelings," She ran a finger down Seth's jaw, "who serve as my... middle management. You and the other underlings answer to them and stay out of my hair. It's all very simple."

"But--" Robin started to say.

"Shut up," Seth said. Robin wanted to scream, but her tongue wouldn't move. The only sound she could make was a low gurgle in the back of her throat.

Nia tapped Seth's chest. "You are *very* lucky that this one happened to wander in tonight after you lost your last one."

Robin stared at the two of them, horror and terror warring in her stomach. *Lost the last one?*

Seth shrugged. "It's not my fault the clients like it rough."

Nia caressed the side of Seth's face and then down to his neck in a gesture that might have been intimate, but looked threatening. "Remember to take better care of your toys, because I'm not always going to keep replacing them."

Seth bowed his head. "Yes, my sire."

Nia pointed to the other robed figure and snapped her fingers. "Rick, you're with me. You're driving me to the spa. I have a facial that starts in an hour." She glanced down at Robin and clicked her tongue. "Have fun with this one. She may need some breaking before she's fit for company." And with that, Nia sashayed out the door.

Seth let out a long breath the moment the door closed behind Nia.

"My sire demands that we have some fun." He loosened his belt and Nia felt the blood drain from her face. "So we're going to have fun."

No, no, no, no, no. Her mouth wouldn't move to make the words. Her heartbeat was so loud, she was sure Seth could hear it.

"What the fuck is it?" Seth shouted towards the door.

The banging wasn't just in her chest, it was also coming from outside.

A hard kick to the door sent it crashing inward, the lock exploding and showering both Seth and Robin with splinters.

Danny Dal burst in, his eyes taking in Robin crouched on the floor, Seth over her.

"What's going on here?" Danny asked, his voice hard.

Robin stared at him. This wasn't the same drunk, irresponsible vampire from the bar, this was someone totally different: Danny's voice was confident, strong, and he held himself straight.

"None of this is your business, Prince," Seth said. "This is between me and my new sireling."

"Sireling?" Danny looked at Robin, his eyes wide with horror. He turned to Robin. "You asked *him*?"

She tried to reply, but the words choked in her throat. She found Danny's eyes and shook her head, grateful Seth had told her to *stay down*, not *don't move*.

She mouthed the words, "Help!" and Danny's mouth compressed into a hard line.

"In the name of King Christopher, and in my capacity as enforcer of his majesty's laws against *hortari* abuse, I command you to release whatever demand you have holding this woman."

Seth smiled. "You have no command over me. My sire is the only one who matters, and her will trumps yours every time."

"All vampires answer to the king." Danny moved further into the room, stepping between Robin and Seth.

"Don't come any closer, or else you'll be responsible for what happens next," Seth said. "Bitch, pick up the knife."

Terror gripped her as his command worked its way into her body. The silver knife Seth had used to cut his arm still lay on the floor next to the altar. Robin's hand moved forward, her fingers grasping the hilt. She kept her eyes on Danny's face, mouthing,

"Stop him. Please, stop him."

"This is your last warning, stop this right now." Danny growled.

Seth smiled wide. "I'm just having fun. Bitch, slice your--"

He didn't finish the word.

Robin blinked. She could move. She still felt woozy and heavy, but she got to her feet on shaking legs.

"What..." her voice trailed off.

A wet mound lay at Seth's feet. A second later, his body tumbled to the ground.

Danny re-holstered a machete against his thigh, the edge covered in blood.

"You cut off his head." Her voice seemed to be coming from far away.

"I stopped him from commanding you to hurt yourself. Robin, I'm so sorry I didn't get here sooner. Are you okay?"

"Yes, I'm..." The room tilted and everything went dark as she fainted away.

DANNY HADN'T TAKEN a complete breath in the three hour-drive back to his safe house with Robin stretched out as comfortably as she could in the back seat. It had been centuries since he'd first been turned, but Danny still remembered the total exhaustion that wracked his body as it transitioned from human to vampire. Robin's turning was certainly more disorienting than most.

I can't believe I let everything get so out of control. Danny couldn't remember the last time he'd blundered an investigation so badly. *This is what I get for dismissing those rumors out of hand.*

Danny pulled into his garage, then delicately carried Robin into the house. He laid her on his bed, taking off her shoes, leaving out clothes for her to change into once she'd woken up, and tucking the blankets around her. *What else can I do?* He went down to the kitchen, pouring himself a glass of blood and leaning his head against the cold counter surface.

He hated how close he'd been to losing her. When Danny first arrived at the Blood Oasis, he'd been amazed by the place. The lights, the music, and the exhilaration that flooded from the human guests were like finding a place he hadn't realized he'd been searching for. The vampire working the bar had been a little hesitant to answer Danny's questions, but she had also been busy serving drinks and doing her job. Before he could thoroughly investigate, Danny found himself surrounded by requests to dance, to check out the upstairs, and was herded into a party room for a horse shifter's bachelorette party of ladies so excited to be in the same room as a vampire; their brays rattled the mirrors on the walls. The horses had been so good-natured with their questions about vampire strength; Danny had barely noticed nearly an hour had passed until he heard Robin's scream from down the hall.

Danny squeezed his eyes shut to try and push away the memory, and the terror, which pricked at the back of his throat when he recognized her voice. *She should be awake by now*, he thought, glancing at the clock. She'd slept an entire day. He grabbed some blood from the fridge, arranging glasses on a tray. *Please, please let her be okay.* He padded up the stairs, wincing at each creak underfoot.

"Shit!" Danny whispered as the tray of glasses clinked against one another. Sometimes it felt like the quieter he tried to be, the louder he ended up being.

"It's okay, I'm awake!" A voice called out from the other side of the heavy wooden door.

Danny grinned. At least she didn't *sound* traumatized. He pushed open the door with one hand and proudly held out the tray in the other. "Breakfast is served."

Robin was at the window, radiant in the moonlight. She had changed into the clothes Danny bought her: jeans and a forest green cable knit sweater that dipped in a tantalizing crescent at her neck.

"How are you?" he asked.

"Better. That smells really good." Robin sniffed the air. "I knew vampires could smell a donor's emotions through their blood, but this is *extraordinary*." She plopped down onto the bed, eyeing the tray.

Danny grinned and set breakfast down on the table next to the bed. When he was first turned, he was a grumpy mess for a week. But of course Robin would be downright *agreeable*. She was a very special brand of tenacious.

"I managed to scrape together a flight of samples for you." He pulled a thin, orange piece of plastic from his pocket. "And a crazy straw."

Robin laughed, and the sound softened the knots of tension along Danny's shoulders. She took the straw delicately from his hand, tracing her fingers along the loops and twists.

"This is perfect." She took his hand in her own and felt her touch all the way up his arm. "Thank you so much for...for everything. I can't believe I was so *stupid*."

He placed his hand over hers. "It's not your fault, it sounds like a lot of people have been drawn in by the Blood Oasis. I was actually there to investigate rumors of *hortari* coercion. I'm just glad I showed up when I did." Danny nudged the tray towards Robin. He fought to keep his expression casual. The memory of what Robin had looked like curled on the floor, her body as still as a corpse, eyes wide with terror, made him want to pull her tight to his chest. Seth's head on the ground wasn't enough. Danny was going to slice through the Blood Oasis like jungle grasses.

Robin dipped her straw into the closest glass and drank deep, her face wrinkled in trepidation. As the liquid disappeared through the loops of the straw, Robin's face lit up, her eyes wide as a slow smile moved its way across her cheeks.

"This tastes like..." She pressed her fingertips against her lips. "Peace."

Danny nodded approvingly. "That donor was meditating when he gave blood. His serene calm is captured in the very cells of what you're drinking." He remembered fondly the first time his sire, Christopher, had presented him a very similar array of blood samples to teach Danny how to enjoy a wide variety of emotions. Danny pushed down a pang of regret. *If only I was as good a sire as Christopher.*

"Peace was a good choice for today. I still can't believe what happened last night." Robin sat back against the stacked pillows on the bed, rolling the glass of blood back and forth between her palms. "I was so naive to go in on my own."

"What *is* going on at that place?" Danny asked.

"The staff there, their movements were so unnatural, their smiles forced. Something just felt...off. It seemed like they didn't want to work there." Robin deposited her now-empty glass back onto the tray. "But when I met Nia Ashmore," Robin shuddered, "and she agreed to turn me, I didn't even *think* about how creepy the staff was acting. From the way she and Seth spoke about their sirelings...they talked about them like disposable toys. I can't believe what could have happened..." Her voice trailed off, her face losing color.

Danny pulled her close, her body fitting against his perfectly. She laid her head on his shoulder.

"We are going to get those sons of bitches," he said into her hair. "We'll stop them from using the *hortari* to make any more slaves."

"Sex slaves." Robin shuddered. "We have to help them, get all of them out of there."

"We will." Danny pulled his phone out of his pocket. "We're going to need help if we're going to take on the entire Blood Oasis. Who knows how many vampires Nia has under her control?"

Danny was shocked when Christopher picked up his

phone after only one ring. The king was usually bogged down by endless meetings and audiences.

"Danny, what's the news?" Christopher sounded anxious.

"Everything we've heard about the Blood Oasis is true." Danny's words flew out in a rush. "The brothel is run by vampires who use *hortari* to force their sirelings to prostitute themselves. I've texted you the address and some photos I managed to take while undercover."

"I feared that might be your report, although I desperately hoped to be wrong this time. Hold on." Christopher's voice muffled as he pulled away from the phone to talk with a female voice Danny recognized as his sireling sister and Christopher's head of security, Margot. "We can send you one hundred of our best soldiers. Because you're so remote, they'll get to your location in forty-eight hours."

"Thank you, Christopher." Danny hung up the phone and turned back to Robin. "We're all set. The king is sending soldiers to break up the Blood Oasis. In two days, the nightmare those vampires are living will be over."

"Just like that?" Robin dunked her straw into another glass of blood and drank deep.

"Christopher is my sire and my king. I trust him."

"I wish *my* sire had been that trustworthy." Robin started giggling, a delicate laugh that trickled its way down a whole octave.

"Robin?" *Is she having some kind of breakdown?*

"Sorry, I'm not laughing at you, it's the blood." She took another sip. "It's so bubbly and happy."

Danny relaxed. "That'll be the pixie, then." Danny laughed. "They're almost always in a great mood. I've never asked why." Danny settled on the bed, looking around the opulent bedroom of high ceilings and modern art Margot had designed for him over the years. The decorations usually brought him comfort, but not today. His mind kept looping back to what Robin had gone through.

"Robin, you deserve an explanation." He took a deep breath. "For why I didn't turn you when you asked the first time."

"No," she put a hand over his. "You don't have to explain yourself to me. I see that you're very upset by what happened, but, with all due respect, how I became a vampire isn't about you. I knew I was taking a risk, and I made the best decision I could with the information I had."

Robin finished the blood and stretched out, her long, lean legs curling past the end of the bed frame. Danny looked at her in amazement. She was one of the strongest women he'd ever met in three hundred years. Danny moved towards the door. If he didn't get out now, he was afraid he would do something rash, like kiss her.

"It's been a long night. You'll need your rest. Christopher's men will bring Nia to justice for what she's done to you. You can relax."

Robin jumped to her feet. "Are you crazy? I'm a *vampire* for goodness sake. I've already rested plenty. Let's have some fun."

"Anxious to try out your new super senses?" Danny asked with a laugh.

"Actually I've got something *much* more interesting in mind." Robin said as she pulled Danny out the door.

ROBIN HOPED she never got over the wonder of her vampire senses. The night had never been so bright, or the smells and sounds so distinct. The breeze against her skin felt like it cocooned her in a whirlwind.

The forest teemed with noise and colors she'd never noticed before, her vampire senses making the night seem as clear as day. She could spot every vultrich pecking in the underbrush in perfect detail.

At her first glance, being able to see them more clearly didn't enhance the vultrich's beauty. They still resembled raptors more than eagles. Their red, scaly heads with oversized, beady eyes and razor-sharp beaks didn't grow more charming now that she could see the detail of every scale and feather. Greater perception couldn't make their long, talon-pointed feet and fluffy wings more graceful.

And yet... the longer she studied them with her vampire senses, she could see details she'd never been able to spot before. So many small beauties she'd missed, like the gloss on their feathers shining with an emerald sheen in the moonlight. The sounds they made to each other had a nuanced complexity she hadn't heard before, with squeaks and squawks outside the range of human hearing, which sounded almost like speech.

She hadn't thought it was possible to love them more.

"So these are what you became a vampire for." Danny shifted his weight beside her. "What's the appeal?"

"Sure, they're not *traditionally* beautiful, but that doesn't mean they don't deserve the chance to live." The words surged forward automatically, too many arguments with contractors and real estate developers bringing the well-rehearsed script to her tongue.

Danny turned to her, eyebrows raised. "That's not what I meant. Why do you fight for *this* particular species? Why aren't you fighting for the rights of the centipede, for example? You had no problem stepping on one when we were hiking up here."

Blood rushed to Robin's face in embarrassment. Centipedes had always creeped her out on a primal level. When a three-inch one had crossed in front of them on the trail, stomping on it was instinctual.

"I *exist* because of these birds, so I feel a sort of responsibility to make sure that they continue to exist too."

"You don't *look* part bird to me." Danny chuckled and stared at Robin, turning his head from side to side. "You're going to have to explain that one." He sat down, leaning against an oak tree and patting the ground for her to join him. "If vultrich have magical life-creation abilities, that's something I'd like to know about."

She chuckled, walked over, and settled beside him on the ground, curling up against his side. On the other side of the nesting area, one of the adults made a warning caw and three of the adults converged to herd the nestlings--balls of grey fluff, feathers, and sharp beaks--into an alcove while the other adults attacked a snake creeping through the grass with sharp efficiency.

"Nothing like that. My mother was a birdwatcher. Well, she was a math teacher, but birdwatching was her love. She took it very seriously, brought a camera with her everywhere she went, and kept detailed logs of every bird she spotted." As Robin talked, the memories unfolded like a video recording, complete with the crinkling sound of the watermarked pages of her mother's journal as they turned, and the rich scent of earth that saturated both the notebook and her mother's hands.

Robin crossed her arms tight against her chest, wondering for the first time since her parents died what had happened to that notebook. It hadn't seemed significant at the time, just a list of bird names next to dates and locations. It had probably been trashed along with everything else that couldn't be donated. Robin inhaled deeply, drinking in the individual fragrances of the moss on the trees, the mushroom at her hip, and each separate leaf on the ground. None of them were quite a match for the smell of her mother's hands.

"And she taught you to like vultrich?" Danny's words brought her back to the present.

"Sort of. That's how she met my dad. He owned a couple vegan restaurants in town and was an avid jogger. He'd joke that he loved being out in the forest because he'd never heard a tree complain that tofu didn't taste like bacon. Dad was out running when my Mom waved a sky worm in the air and accidentally drew a flock of vultrich down on herself."

Robin smiled at the memory. She could almost feel the weight and smoothness of the plastic container in her hands from when her mother first showed Robin her stash of sky worms.

Be careful with these, my Robin, she'd said as she carefully lifted the edge of the lid off, making the tiniest of holes for the scent of the sky worm to escape. *They may not seem tasty to you and me, but sometimes the most potent obsessions come in the smallest packages.*

The day Robin's parents met, her mother was still new to nocturnal birds and had only read about how vultrich were drawn to sky worms. To try and find one, she'd waved a sky worm in the air above her head like a tiny flag. When the swarm descended on her, it was all Robin's mother could do to drop the worm and run like hell as the sharp-beaked carnivores raced after the lingering scent of the worms on her fingertips. With her focus mostly on the enormous birds racing after her, she'd smashed into Robin's father running at full tilt.

At her scream for him to "Run!", they'd grabbed hands and sprinted out of the trees and to the safety of his truck parked nearby. Once the flock departed, Robin's dad had asked for the birdwatcher's number, and they'd never stopped running hand in hand together through the world, even up to the very end.

Robin smiled. "Mom always said she would have fallen head over heels for him no matter the circumstances, but it was the vultrich who gave her the right incentive."

"What do your parents think about your vultrich crusade?" Danny asked.

"I don't know, but I hope they're proud of me, wherever they are." The car crash that took them away five years ago felt just as raw as when she'd first gotten the phone call from the hospital.

We're so sorry to tell you this, miss, but we have some bad news...

She blinked away tears, hoping Danny hadn't seen.

"They took me on birdwatching trips every summer to look at the vultrich. Between Mom's teaching during the day and Dad having to man the restaurants in the evening, making time to go vultrich watching together are my favorite memories of when we were all together."

She fought against the flood of memories crashing down on her. Year after year of sitting against trees just like this one, her head nestled under her mother's arm as her father kissed her hair, all of them watching the slow pecking of the birds, pointing out when one made a particular cry, or a baby vultrich got loose underfoot. Robin once left an open container of sky worms in the family car, and a flock had broken every window and totaled the exterior trying to get in. Her parents just laughed, telling Robin it was a small price to pay for the vultrich's happiness.

Danny put his hand over hers. "Remembering everything like you're reliving it, it gets easier over time."

"How? It's all so much." And there, just lurking behind all the memories of her parents, were the more recent, ugly memories she never wanted to relive again. Nia's hands pushing the cup of Seth's blood toward her mouth. The smooth handle of the knife in her hand, her helpless terror seeing her own hand drawing the blade closer to her neck with no way to stop it. The thump of Seth's head landing on the floor, the sound of each drop of blood dripping off of Danny's machete.

"Robin? It's going to be okay." Danny's hands were on her shoulders, his grip loose and soothing. His touch brought her back to the present, sights and sounds around her coming into focus. One male vultrich pecked tentatively on the wing feathers of the female vultrich next to him, making small, plaintive noises.

"Exactly *how* is this going to be okay?" Robin gazed into his deep, brown eyes. "My birds' habitat is shrinking by the day. There are people being tortured and stripped of their will and we're just sitting here--"

He got to his feet, holding out a hand to help her up. "We move forward, that's what we do."

Robin fought the urge to roll her eyes. *As if it's that easy.* He didn't let go of her hand as they walked together away from the birds and back toward where they'd parked the car.

"We save your birds, we get justice for the assholes who hurt you, and you'll learn to live in the moment." He shrugged. "It's hard for a lot of us. But Christopher's wife,

Alice, was turned recently too. She's an artist, always looking at the world around her, living pretty much perpetually in the present. The temptation to relive memories doesn't call to her. I'd forgotten how hard it is in the beginning to push the reveries away."

"It was hard for you too?"

Danny chuckled. "Yes, but that's mostly because I didn't try. I thought that the ability to pull up such clear memories all of the time was one of the prime perks of being a vamp. When I was turned about three hundred years or so ago, I wanted to map out the whole world. Christopher found me when I'd already been living in the deep jungle of what's now India for five years, and he thought I had the potential to make the world a better place if I had more time to live in it. Considering I was a hard-drinking and self-acknowledged rogue in those days, he saw a lot more potential in myself than I ever did."

He grinned at Robin and she blushed to her hair. Danny was a little too easy to visualize as a nineteenth century Indiana Jones-type, cutting a swath through the undergrowth with his machete. Getting sweaty. Maybe taking a skinny dip in a stream...

She shook herself. *What was it about Danny that was so completely distracting?* As they walked through the woods, she was hyper-aware of every place their bodies brushed, his palm pressed against hers. The smallest jostle of their hips against each other aroused her past anything she'd ever felt before.

His smile dropped a little. "The thing about being an explorer is that it isn't just being on the hunt for something that's never been found before, it's about comparing everything you see to what you've already experienced." He chuckled and shrugged. "I was making a hand-drawn map of the whole world, but it took me so long to get anywhere, by the time I'd looped back to a place I'd already been, it had changed completely. And for a long time, I loved that. Every time I swung by Constantinople, it was like a totally different city, with new temples and then churches and then temples again, the streets and people all changed and I gave up trying to keep track." He glanced at Robin. "I also realized how much of the present I was missing. Always thinking about the past was like living in a dream."

She nodded, remembering the strange disconnect of sitting against the tree watching the vultrich beside Danny while also living a dozen other memories of being beside her parents. How easy would it be, in the centuries to come, to simply relive past moments rather than making new memories?

No. I can't fall down that trap.

She didn't look back at the forest when they reached Danny's truck, concentrating on what was in front of her. His truck needed a thorough cleaning--the rubber mat on the floor was impacted with mud and fast food crumbs, with tissues crammed into the side pockets along with what looked like a plastic army toy--but smelled overwhelmingly like Danny. It was a pleasant smell, one that made it easy for her to rest her head back in the seat and let her body curve into the cushions.

Danny glanced at her as he maneuvered the truck into gear, his mouth thinning. "Are you going to be okay alone at my place? I can take you back to your house if you want."

"Where will you be?" she asked.

"I know the cavalry isn't coming in until the day after tomorrow, but I was thinking of heading back to the Blood

Oasis. Christopher will need more information before they go in. I'm going to map out all the possible entry points and exits, the dimensions of the hallways, and plan an effective route in and out."

"I want to come too." The thought of going back to that place filled her with a chest-chilling terror, but if Danny was going back there, then she was too. The thought of him sleuthing around that hellhole while she relaxed in his Jacuzzi wasn't an option.

"You don't have the training. I've been doing this kind of investigating for hundreds of years."

"I need to do this. You know what they did to me. If there's *any* way I can help take them down, I'm going to do it."

He sighed, looking over at her. Robin kept her face carefully calm, with a determined set of her jaw so he would know she meant business. His hands clenched and unclenched around the steering wheel.

"Fine. I could use some backup." He looked her over again, his expression speculative. "But you can't go back there looking like that."

Robin looked down at herself. The jeans and sweater that Danny had provided when she woke up didn't exactly blend into a vampire club. Nia would definitely be out for Robin and Danny's blood after Seth's beheading.

"What did you have in mind?"

Looking into Danny's closet was like walking onto the set of a Mission Impossible porn parody. Rows of leather chaps and wicked-looking ribbon-laced corsets in men and women's sizes lined both sides, along with enough toys to fill two Amsterdam sex shops.

"How many whips does one man need?" Robin asked.

Danny grinned. "Most of these were gifts. My friends know I'm a collector."

"So, not *just* a world explorer, then?" Robin raised her eyebrows at him.

"Is anyone ever just one thing?"

Danny grabbed a black bra off a rack and held it up in front of Robin, tilting his head before putting it back and tossing her one with slightly larger cups. She didn't need to glance at the label to know the new one would fit perfectly.

"Let's say that I'm always down to try new things." He winked at her.

Hot damn. The man's winks were nuclear-powered. Just the movement of his eyelid had arousal surge between her legs. Heat filled her to her toes.

He strolled deeper into the closet, making little noises like he was running into old friends as he pulled back one hanger to take a better look at a pair of chaps with three-inch fringe on the side, and then caress a pair of blood-red knee-high boots with four-inch sparkling heels. For a second, she could picture him wearing the entire rig and the effect was irresistible.

Everything he does is sexy, Robin thought. *Good thing he's not my sire*. But she shut down that line of thought before she could think too hard on sires. Despite how awful the moment of her turning had been, she was grateful her sire was dead. She was free. Utterly free.

If she wanted to walk away from helping Danny take down Nia and the Blood Oasis, she could.

If she wanted to go explore the deep jungles of the world and forget the vultrich and every heartbreaking and warming memory she had...she could.

She was a vampire: a strong, fast, emotion-reading, blood-drinking immortal. Everything had been so crazy since she was turned she hadn't had a chance to sit back and appreciate that she'd *done* it. She'd gotten a vampire to turn her! Now she had all the time in the world to figure out what to do with herself.

Robin stalked forward into the closet, grabbing every costume piece that caught her eye. She remembered her joy when she first walked into the Blood Oasis, how the place promised a fantasy of freedom and fun. No matter how Nia had perverted that promise, Robin could live the life she chose.

Black corset that pushed her breasts sky-high? *Check*. Fishnet stockings held up by a garter belt? *Check*. Lace gloves inset with rubies that stretched up past her elbows? *Check*. A dab of body glitter between her breasts to draw the eye, along with eye liner drawn on so thick and bold it would make her mother tremble in her grave? *Check and check*.

Robin inspected her reflection. Nia definitely wouldn't recognize her. *Robin* barely recognized the sexy and confident woman in the mirror. She bared her fangs, tossing back her hair and letting her canines extend to dip into her lower lip. The vampire in the mirror looked ready to tear Nia's throat out, and anyone else who tried to stand in her way. She growled, smiling at the effect. The next time a contractor called her a "tree-hugging hippie" to get her to move from where she blocked his access to a nest, he was going to get quite a shock.

"Hot damn," Danny said behind her. His eyes roamed up and down her body like he couldn't get enough.

"Hot damn yourself."

Danny hadn't been idle while she was getting dressed. His

leather pants were so tight they could have been painted on, and he wore a silk vest with nothing underneath, open to display acres of tight muscles and a truly drool-worthy set of abs. He caught her eye and raised one perfect eyebrow, his grin turning smug.

"Like what you see?" he asked.

She stalked forward, running her fingernails along the side of the fabric, tickling the soft skin along his pecs and down to his stomach. "I'm an environmentalist. I can always appreciate a fine natural specimen."

"Uh huh." He skimmed his fingers along her shoulders, caressing the top of her gloves where the fabric met the sensitive skin on the inside of her arm. To her enhanced senses, every brush of his fingers electrified, sizzling across her skin. He kissed her neck and she heated like a furnace burned in her lower belly, radiating out.

"As a former explorer, I just love discovering..." Danny's hands skated down her spine over her corset to land squarely on her ass. "New territories."

He dropped to his knees, nudging her legs apart and kissing a trail of nips and licks up her inner thigh, unhooking the garter belt to trace the edge of her fishnet stockings with his tongue.

"Oh yes," she panted. Danny grinned, his dimples filled with mischief as his fingers played with the ticklish skin behind her knees and along the back of her thigh. She grabbed the wall beside her for balance as her legs threatened to give way, her hand closing around a vibrator along a shelf. It was shaped like an egg, the buttons along the side alerting it to buzzing life as she picked it up.

"Ooo, good thought," Danny's fingers probed under the lace panties fully on display to caress down the crease between her ass. He plucked the egg from her fingers and tucked it into her panties so the elastic would hold it against her clit as his tongue traced tantalizing circles along her inner thighs so close, yet never close enough, to her core.

"More." Her breath came in rapid pants. "I need more."

The warm buzzing of the vibrator sent shooting pleasure down her legs.

"Holy crap!" she yelped as he pulled aside the piece of lace between her legs and plunged his tongue inside of her.

"Delicious," he murmured, tapping the egg so its force increased to maximum.

Her first orgasm hit so suddenly, her upper body convulsed against the wall, her head knocking aside a stack of harnesses and her scream echoing around the closet. She sagged against the clothes, already lightheaded.

He carefully withdrew the egg. "Having fun yet?"

"Oh, we're just starting." She grabbed his shirt, pulling it over his head and throwing it on the floor. Her lips fastened around his nipples, loving their pert tautness and his guttural groan as she lightly nibbled along the tips. Everything from his rugged smell, to the smoothness of his skin was more incredible than anything she'd ever felt before.

Feathers on the shelf next to her brushed against her face and it was so unexpected, she startled away, leaning instinctively closer into Danny. His arm closed around her. She tilted her head back in invitation and he dove for her lips, devouring her with abandon, sucking and fucking her mouth with his tongue. Still sensitive after her last orgasm, the sensations were too much and not enough, her hips desperately pushing closer to his until she felt the hard iron of his erection pressing against her stomach.

He bit a trail of kisses along her chin up to her ear,

nibbling along the lobe. She hadn't thought anything so gentle could send her hormones racing again so fast, but her knees were on the verge of giving out under her. She grasped his shoulders with one hand to stay upright, the other beginning to unfasten his belt, her fingers clumsy in her speed to get all of his clothes off.

He yanked down his pants, his massive cock begging to be licked and caressed.

Robin slid seductively to the ground, letting her hands run down the length of Danny's chest. Her fingers played in the grooves of his abs until she reached her destination.

"My turn," she murmured.

She stared down at the hard length pulsing with desire for her, and Robin smiled at his enthusiastic response. She closed her hand around him, making Danny buck forward, eager for her touch. Robin licked a winding road along his shaft, taking her time with him, growing ever wetter as she tasted the precum that glistened on his tip.

Robin slid him inside her mouth and Danny let out a low groan as she teased his cock with her tongue, bobbing relentlessly. She slid her hands along his thighs, his ass, his balls. Everything about him felt right in her hands, each new sound of pleasure he made increasing the arousal surging between her legs and along her limbs.

Danny tensed, about to cum, and Robin released him with a pop. *No need to end the fun quite yet.*

"Is it too corny to tell you that you're the most beautiful and amazing being I've seen in centuries and I--"

Robin yanked down her panties, putting her hand over his mouth. "Show me. Fuck me right now."

She needed him: dirty, urgent, and surrounded by costumes, sex toys, and reminders of the whole new world she'd joined. She leaned over the top of a wooden trunk in the bottom of the closet, spreading her legs wide.

"Thank fuck," he cried.

"Yes!" She thrust her hips back just in time to feel his hands on her ass and the head of his cock slip between her wet folds. He was so big, he stretched her channel, and she moaned at the perfection of it. He slid in slow, giving her time to accommodate his size.

"I don't want you to be delicate," Robin commanded. "I'm a fucking vampire. Pound me, Danny."

"Yes, my love." He said the last so low she wasn't sure he heard him right, but by then, she couldn't think straight. He'd lifted her up so her feet no longer touched the ground, changing the angle so he could pull her forward with each stroke, withdrawing nearly all the way out before slamming back in over and over.

Danny pounded into her mercilessly and she loved every second of it. He hit every amazing spot inside, sending thrills of fireworks and building pulsing heat down to her curling toes.

Her breasts pressed against the hard top of the chest, the friction of the wood against the silken inside of the corset she still wore playing gentle havoc with her breasts and nipples. He shifted his weight so his arm held up her hips and he could use one hand to reach under her and play with her clit, squeezing and rubbing it just enough to send her over the edge.

"Yes! Yes, yes, yes, yes," she screamed over and over as she rode the wave of pleasure erupting through her. Fireworks of pleasure burst along her spine, her toes curled, and her fingers clenched tight around the edge of the chest so hard the wood splintered in between her knuckles. A second later, she felt his cock expand inside her as he shuddered over her, moaning low.

She collapsed against the top of the trunk, breathing heavily as Danny's cock softened inside her and he withdrew. Nothing had ever been so intense, so perfect. She glanced behind her at her vampire lover, who had slid down to the floor. His grin was so wide, it lit up the dark corners of the closet.

The floor around him was strewn with their clothing. Her cheeks itched where eye-liner had mixed with sweat and dripped down her face.

She laughed. "It looks like we're going to have to get ready all over again."

Danny's laugh echoed hers, sitting up to cradle her face between her hands and kiss her gently. He pulled her back against him so they were cuddled together under the rack of chaps.

"Worth it. Worth every second."

Robin sank back into his embrace, loving the feel of his arms around her, the peace and perfection of being beside him. *Forever with him is more than I ever dreamed of*, she thought as she breathed in the lush smell of his sweat mixed with tanned leather. *If he hadn't saved me when he did...*

Seyah and the other vampires under Nia's will were all still there. It was like an itch at the back of her mind. Even as she lay in Danny's arms in perfect harmony, they were trapped there. *How many horrors have they already experienced tonight because we were distracted?*

She tapped Danny's shoulder. "We need to get to work."

He caught the seriousness in her tone and nodded. "Let's go."

How a place so lovely could hide such ugliness, Danny would never understand. Even the back door had a certain charm about it, framed with rose bushes. From his crouched position to the left of the door--out of range of the security cameras--he could hear swishes of movement coming from inside. He'd sent a quick text to Margot telling her he was headed to the club to gather intel and her response had been less than encouraging: a series of curses and angry emoticons telling him to wait for the professionals, and stay put until they arrived. But he couldn't stay still. Not when that haunted look came over Robin's face and he knew there were so many others that they'd both left behind at the Blood Oasis. He *had* to help.

Footsteps thumped inside and he froze, the movement tightening his leather getup in ways that were not entirely unpleasant. Danny held his breath as he followed the sound of footsteps growing louder, and then fading away.

He let out a breath and pulled his lock picking tools from one of his boots. Kneeling with the lock at eye level, he selected a long, silver hook, and his smallest torsion wrench. He moved slowly, hoping the enhanced hearing of the vampires inside would be focused on the ecstatic moans of their guests rather than the incriminating sounds of metal scraping against metal.

The soft click of success made him grin, and he slipped inside without a sound. The back areas of the Blood Oasis were less extravagant than the front, but still stunning. The hallways were lined with antique gas lamps which glowed warmer than modern appliances could ever achieve, and the windows' heavy, black, curtains shown with a velvet sheen. The red carpeting would put a movie premiere to shame.

Somewhere out front, Robin was doing her own recon dressed like the best part of every wet dream he'd ever had. The memory of Robin's sated expression after he pounded her into oblivion gave Danny's wild grin some authenticity as he walked down the hallway, providing his best imitation of an excited patron. He counted his steps as he moved, occasionally stretching out wide in a faux yawn to get a feel for the width of the corridor, drawing a map in his mind. The more information he could provide to Christopher's police, the more successful their raid would be.

A vampire with a vacant expression concealed under a thick blanket of makeup giggled and tossed her hair at an older satyr who leaned heavily on her, wobbling on his small, cloven hoofs. They careened back and forth like a pin-ball as the woman struggled to hold the man's drunken, stout form upright.

"You look lovely as ever tonight, my dear," he slurred, his tiny hand gliding down to cup the woman's ass. She couldn't quite hide her wince fast enough and Danny wondered how he had missed these signs the first time he was here.

She giggled. "I wanted to look my best for you, sweetie." Her gaze caught on Danny's and her eyes widened in recognition before quickly turning away.

It was the scared, beseeching look in her eyes that did it, her brown eyes too similar to Robin's. Danny turned back. "Do you need help?" He whispered. "I can get you out of here."

"You picked the wrong night to sneak around," she whispered back as she gave up trying to keep the satyr upright and he slipped down to the floor and began to gently snore.

"There's a big event happening, security has been bumped up to keep anyone from escaping once they find their candidates."

"They're making new vampires tonight?" *Robin's out there alone, she doesn't know.* His stomach churned.

"It's a big gala to get the naive and beautiful in here," she whispered fast. The satyr was beginning to come around, blinking and groaning at the light from the candles. "You gotta leave. Now."

"Not until I get what I need."

"They're in the dungeons," she hissed. Louder, to the satyr she cooed, "Oh sweetie face, are you okay? You look like you need another drink." She picked up the satyr like an oversized doll and carried him back in the direction they came, away from the marked bedrooms.

Danny stared after her a long moment. *They're in the dungeons? What does that mean?* It was the best lead he had.

He picked up a dank scent and followed it straight down to the dungeon. It was more decorative than threatening, but solid all the same. Rows of metal doors lined the long, dead-end hallway, each too thick for sound to come through. It was also cold, even for a vampire, and Danny wished he had selected an ensemble that left more to the imagination. The walls were painted a shiny black, with electric candle sconces spaced in intimate alcoves with padded sides, perfect for getting swept up and fucked against the wall.

Danny caught the steady red light of a security camera out of the corner of his eye. Danny knew the model, an ACE-457, consisting of a single steady camera in a small black dome protruding from the ceiling. *Hardly subtle.* He scoffed and rolled to the ground, easily maneuvering into the camera's blind spot as he made his way forward.

The long hallway was separated in to dozens of cells. Each was outfitted with a single sliding window. Danny shrugged. *Some people like to watch.* Danny peeked in a few. Some of the cells were decked out for recreational purposes, filled with a creative array of chains and BDSM paraphernalia. But as Danny made his way towards the cells in the back, he bit back a shudder. Marks that looked like scratches from human fingernails dug along the walls, and splatters of blood that reeked with fear covered the floor. *This isn't just a sex dungeon.*

The ground shook as heavy footsteps approached. *Shit! Just what I need.* Danny ducked into an open cell and froze. He held his breath, and tried to slow the frantic beating of his heart.

Danny quickly peered around the corner of the cell, and cursed himself for getting cornered so easily. The walls, floor, and ceiling were reinforced iron even vampire strength couldn't break. The exit, and only escape, was blocked by a mountain of a vampire, all muscle and no neck. The mountain was glaring into the cells, clearly looking for something. *Has he seen me?*

The answer appeared in the form of a large hand lifting him off the ground and throwing him against the cell wall.

I'll take that as a 'yes'. Danny planted his hands on the floor and kicked the mountainous vampire in the solar plexus with all his might. He used the momentum from the kick to complete his movement into a flip, landing on his feet. Free in the hallway, he sprinted for stairs, pushing at the limit of his vampiric speed so the walls passed in a blur. Shouted curses from the vamp followed at his heels. With a grin, Danny dropped to the ground, slid across the cold floor, and threw open the last iron cell door just in time for his pursuer to slam into it at full speed. The distinctly vampire-shaped dent in the door was comically satisfying.

"Smooth," came a low voice Danny least wanted to hear. He spun to face his only exit. Nia Ashmore glanced over at the dented door and grinned at Danny from several steps up, flanked on either side by axe-wielding vampires. "Just because you dodged the visible security cameras, doesn't mean you weren't picked up on the hidden ones. I know *everything* that goes on here." She tsked. "Prince Dal, I presume? It's too bad you've become so knowledgeable of my organization."

"King Christopher knows of your abuses!" Danny spat. "You're finished."

"Am I?" Nia mockingly brought a thin hand to her chest. "Oh my." She rolled her eyes.

"You will not disrespect the king!" Hot rage flooded Danny's vision.

"That sire of yours is no king of mine. I don't know if he doesn't respect the *hortari,* or is just too pathetic to use it, but..." She crooked her finger forward, and her two guards brought their axes down to Danny's throat. "Let's just say I know how to *deal* with weakness."

Danny braced himself for the killing blow, defiantly staring Nia down. He took a deep breath and readied himself for oblivion.

"Lock him to the dungeons, boys," Nia said. "Since you like my holding cells so much, you'll get to enjoy the rest of your miserable existence in one. If the king knows about us, then having his sireling as a hostage will be lovely leverage." She wrinkled her nose. "Also I don't need vampire all over my nice floor."

The axes retreated from his neck as thick chains clinked

around Danny's wrists. Robin's smile flashed before his eyes, and Danny nearly lost his footing. *No!* Robin was in danger. He'd *led* her to this place. Surely, Nia would spot her in the crowd, especially now that she'd found Danny. Everything was spiraling out of control. A heavy hand pushed him forward, arms clamped around his shoulders dragging him back toward the blood-soaked, back cells.

Robin, my love, he prayed to whoever might be listening. *Please be okay.*

SOMETHING WAS WRONG. Danny should have been back by now. They'd agreed that after he finished his map, they'd meet here. Robin did a third lap of the Blood Oasis, and still no Danny. Being here again, she was struck by how beautiful and amazing this place *could* be. A better DJ, a touch of softer lighting, staff who actually *consented* to work there...it was the little things that could have made this place an empowering retreat of sex and fun.

What would really make it perfect is if she could find Danny.

"Are you here for the Star Mixer?" a cheetah shifter in a pinstripe suit asked, handing her a flyer.

Robin stopped short, remembering her role as casual party-goer and twirled the end of her hair with her finger. "No. I just came for the fun!" She looked down at the flyer and bit back a gasp.

"I hope we cater to your fantasies!" The man chirped happily before bounding away to approach a woman wearing too much makeup who had just arrived.

Join us for an exciting night full of eternal possibility! Read the front of the flyer in bold letters. The signs she'd passed near the front door made more sense now. The black tie networking affair for aspiring actors and models promised "strength, poise, and the opportunity to proclaim your beauty to the masses." *Nia must be shopping for replacements for the vamps freed when Seth lost his head.* Nothing in the pamphlet mentioned vampires. *Do these people even know what they're being recruited for?*

Robin's stomach churned as she noticed the signage scattered around the Blood Oasis. They had a few hours before the event started, but the staff was already setting up. *No fucking way am I going to let that happen.*

A vampire with a diamond nose ring and a thin-lipped smile leaned against the bar. The woman's eyes widened when she caught Robin's and turned abruptly away. Concerned, Robin came closer.

"I'm under orders to report you to my sire if I see you, Robin," she said fast, stepping back. "But my sire didn't specify *when* I had to report it."

Robin didn't question how the woman knew her name. Danny had killed one of Nia's sirelings for Robin's sake. Both of their names and faces were probably well known by now.

Robin shook her head. "No, but help is coming. I'm here with a friend, we're--"

"Don't tell me anything." The woman looked around quickly, but the folks around them were occupied either dancing or making out. "Look, I'm not allowed to help you. But..." she stopped, considered her words carefully. "Unrelated - did you know that this place has a dungeon? You look like you'd be into our *special* pleasures we offer down there. If you want to check it out, you're going to want to take the second door on the right and..." She rattled off a complex list of directions. Robin grabbed a napkin off the bar and a pen and started to draw a map off of what she described. The woman examined the map and then nodded, her face strained as she skirted the edge of disobeying a *hortari*. Robin kissed the woman's cheek.

"We're going to get you out of here," Robin whispered.

"And I hope we've catered to all your fantasies," the woman replied mechanically.

Robin nodded and slid open the door to the right. There were a few close calls in the hallways, but most of Nia's managers seemed to have better things to do than police the halls. Most of the other vampires she saw turned their heads away and started chatting loudly to whoever they were with about something else. A swelling of pride pushed its way up Robin's chest. No matter what compulsion these poor vampires were under, they found ways to resist.

I'm going to come back for you, she promised silently to their retreating forms.

The smells from the dungeon were overwhelming: sweat, fear, and sex surrounded her to form an impenetrable cloud. She coughed and tried pinching her nose, but it was no use. The sweat and sex smells weren't bad, but the stink of fear made her skin itch.

She slid aside each cell's small, eye-level viewing window as quietly as possible. In one, Robin found a man strapped to a hanging cross groaning in pleasure as a woman encased head to toe in leather whipped him across the ass. In another, a gay couple writhed together in handcuffs.

Where the hell is Danny? There were only two cells left.

Even with enhanced vampire senses, the second-to-last room was so dark, she could barely see the occupants: two men and two women with their arms and legs shackled to the floor in tight balls that barely allowed them to move at all. They were all gagged silent, thick ropes lashed to each of their mouths. *What the hell?* She tried the door, but it was locked shut.

At the sound of her jiggling the latch, the closest man turned to look at her, rage in his narrowed eyes. He pulled at his chains, a muffled scream around the rope echoing around his gag. She recognized him immediately: Seyah.

"Were you one of Seth's vampires?" she whispered through the bars.

He nodded emphatically, hunching over his elbow to point to the others tied up in the cell as well. When Danny killed Seth, his compulsion over his other sirelings was also broken. *My vampire brothers and sisters.* Robin looked around the empty hallway for a key. There was no sign of one and no one around, but that was no guarantee that someone wasn't going to come down at any moment to check on the other guests. Even if she knew how to pick a lock, there was no time to try.

"I will come back for you," she whispered through the door, keeping the eye slot open so they could at least have a little light.

She slid open the window into the last cell. Her heart did a little backflip at the sight of Danny picking a thick padlock using his elongated canine teeth. He was wrapped in so many padlocks and chains, he might as well have been blanketed in them. The locks he'd already unlocked were at least fifty deep on the ground next to him.

"Danny!" She hissed through the door.

He dropped the lock he was currently working on and glared at her.

"What are you doing down here? It's too dangerous!" He

immediately dove back for the lock, flicking open the latch with his teeth and going for the next one. It hit its fellow with a low chunk.

"And what are you going to do once you've gotten out of there?" She cocked an eyebrow at him.

"I need to stop tonight's event. Nia's hosting a gala in just a few hours that's going to enslave a *lot* more vampires. We don't have time to wait for Christopher's army to arrive tomorrow." Another lock hit the pile.

"I know. But we don't need to wait for an army." She pointed to the cell next to him. "We have back up right here."

"What?"

"Seth's sirelings are next door," Robin said.

Danny threw another lock against the pile. "So close?" Another lock down. "At least *one* thing is going right with this mission."

Danny worked this way through the locks as she explained to the bound vampires next door about the royal army coming soon to take this place apart.

"You don't have to help. It's going to be risky, but we could use your support."

Seyah and the rest nodded more quickly than she'd hoped. Once Danny got his own door open, he picked open the neighboring door as well, using his lockpicks now that his hands were free until all four of Seth's sirelings were blinking and stretching in their cell.

"How many vampires do Nia and her sirelings control?" Danny asked once they were all free.

"There's twenty here," said the woman closest. She was rubbing her wrists where the shackles had held her down, her expression murderous. "Divided up among Nia's three remaining sireling managers."

"What are we going to do about *Nia*?" asked the other male vampire, saying the woman's name like a curse.

"I can take care of Nia," Danny said. When they all started arguing at once, Danny held up his hands. "I know you all want your revenge, but Nia is older than you, which makes her stronger. You're not going to be a match for her if it comes down to a fight."

There were plenty of grumbles, but eventually they agreed.

"We still have her three guys in charge to take care of," Robin pointed out, which made everybody perk up. "You all know this place better than we do. How do we get twenty compulsion-controlled vamps contained without anybody getting hurt?"

Watching them plan the best approach reminded Robin of the vultrich herding their nestlings to shelter while their mates tore apart snakes with their beaks. She wasn't sure if Danny would appreciate being compared to her birds, but the thought made her smile. The vampires were protecting their nest, no matter what it took.

They split into three groups, each focused on tracking down and either killing or disabling one of Nia's sirelings. One was easy to find: Rick was in a four-way with two female guests and one of his conscripted vamps, a guy with an eyebrow ring and a buzz cut, kneading Rick's shoulders from behind. Rick was thoroughly distracted, but Robin caught the other vamp's eye through the window with ease. Robin could tell the moment he recognized Seyah and the other of Seth's freed vamps in the hallway behind her. His eyes widened, and he smiled wide, his hands encircling Rick's neck and squeezing hard. Rick passed out before the two guests realized anything was wrong. The vamp said something to them and they smiled, winked at him, and then continued making out with one another. He approached the door and nodded to Seyah.

"Got a knife out here I could borrow? He's only going to be out a few minutes. This asshole needs a beheading."

Seyah started to hand him a weapon he'd picked up from one of the dungeon rooms, but Danny grabbed his hand.

"No, just get them out of there and lock him up." Danny handed the vampire a long length of chain he'd brought up from the dungeon. "The king can put him on trial when he arrives."

"That's not nearly as satisfying," the vampire grumbled, but he bound up the unconscious Rick and hefted him onto his shoulder, giving them all a wink as he headed down to the dungeons.

Two to go.

Robin followed behind as the growing group of liberated vamps searched the hallway for Nia's remaining sirelings, all the while herding guests away into rooms where they could be safely locked away. The second sireling, Jerry, got clubbed over the head and dragged into a room before he recognized Seth's vamps shouldn't be on his floor, while the last, Morty, they found in the middle of the dance floor.

Robin froze, uncertain how to move forward without endangering so many bystanders. One of Seth's vamps, Dulcia, jumped forward to yell, "Sex party in the dungeon!" at the top of her lungs, then motioned for everyone follow her like a scantily-clad pied piper. As the entire dance floor moved downstairs, Morty got swept along in the commotion and was locked in the first cell they could shove him into.

Even with all of Nia's goons taken care of, Danny still looked worried.

Robin touched his arm. "Have you seen any sign of Nia?"

Danny shook his head. "She *has* to be upstairs, it's the only place we haven't looked."

Seyah had found them some blueprints of the building. The upstairs was even more of a maze than the lower floors, purposefully constructed to limit movements and confuse anyone not familiar with the layout.

"Nia's probably in her suite." Seyah pointed to the largest room on the blueprints.

"You're going to need help," Robin said.

He shook his head. "I need you to get everybody out of here. If she makes it past me, I don't want to give her the chance to hurt anybody."

Robin didn't like it, but Danny's logic made sense. Her vampire prince pulled her in for a crushing kiss, his hands cupping her face perfectly. Before she could say anything, he was gone, racing up the stairs.

DANNY FOUGHT against the worry itching at the back of his neck. Robin had proven how remarkably brave and resourceful she was, but she wasn't a warrior. If Nia got away from him, Robin and the other newly-sired vamps would be practically defenseless. He tried to push the thought away so he could focus on the task at hand.

Just don't let her get past you, he told himself, clamping down on any doubts. With a yell, Danny kicked down the gilded door of Nia's suite.

"It's over!" He adjusted his grip on his machete, scanning the room for any sign of the Blood Oasis's evil mistress. Nia's white and gold room was even worse than Danny anticipated.

Furs of endangered species covered the floor, and gold-plated statues of Nia's face topped marble columns. One wall was decorated entirely with murals of her face, while another was a giant, floor-to-ceiling mirror. Light danced off the shining blades of two white-handled axes crossed above the fireplace's mantle.

Nia was beside her enormous bed packing a leather duffel bag overflowing with cash and jewels. She stopped short at the sight of Danny.

"You." She spat.

"Me." Danny twirled his machete. "We've subdued your minions." He stepped towards Nia. "The king knows what you've done." He pointed his machete at her. "You're out of options. Come quietly, or in pieces."

"Honey, do you hear that helicopter?" The sounds of whirring blades grew louder with her every word. "I'm *never* out of options." Moving quicker than a blink, Nia dropped her bag, leapt to the mantle, and grabbed the axes off the wall.

"Fuck!" Danny dropped to the ground, one of her axes whizzing past where his throat had been less than a second before.

Nia bellowed as she leapt off the mantle, swinging her other axe overhead with deadly aim at Danny. He rolled fast, avoiding her axe just as the weapon buried deep into the carpeting.

"I so rarely get to do my own dirty work." Nia purred. She yanked the axe from the floor "I forgot how much fun it can be."

Danny danced back, holding his machete protectively in front of himself, circling her warily.

She was so fast, she had to be old. Really old. The only

chance he had to was to keep her distracted, hopefully take her by surprise. "I'm surprised you can do *anything* on your own. Do your minions wipe your ass for you, too?"

Nia smiled and Danny was instantly reminded that gorillas only grinned as a threat. "My minions do whatever I tell them to do. Which is more than I can say for your worthless sire who lets his raggedy mutts disrupt my business."

"Christopher is worth a thousand of you." With a grunt, Danny kicked the massive wooden bed at Nia, the two-hundred pound piece of furniture hurtling through the air toward her. A deafening clatter ripped through the room as the bed exploded, and Nia emerged from the dust between two cleaved halves of the bed, axe-first.

"That bed belonged to Stalin!" she yelled. "Do you know what that thing *cost,* you asshole!"

Danny charged, holding his machete high. He swung his blade in a wide arc, changing the angle at the last second so Nia dodged directly into the path of his weapon. She cried out as the blade sliced across her shoulder, leaving a thin trail of blood behind.

Danny sniffed the air, now pungent with Nia's emotions from her spilled blood. She was *furious.* He grinned. *I can use that.*

Danny dodged back from her rage-fueled axe swing, his chest just out of Nia's reach. "Some master criminal you are."

Nia's blade whipped through the empty air without making contact, her frustration and rage growing with each swing.

"Fuck this." Nia jumped backward, grabbing one of her golden busts and pitching it with the crack of a fastball directly at his head. Danny swerved to avoid the missile and yelped as her axe swing came down directly into his path.

Oh, shit. Danny moved to block the axe's blow, managing to catch her blade deep into his forearm. The block managed to throw Nia off balance just enough to break her momentum and allow Danny to roll away. He swung his machete at her, driving it into the wooden handle of the axe. With the machete stuck in the axe's shaft, they were caught together. Each struggled against the blade of the each other. For one second, Danny remembered Blagfor, the way his rocklike arms bristled as he pushed against Danny's hand. It hadn't been a fair fight. And Danny didn't have to fight fair.

He kicked Nia hard in the stomach, shooting her across the room and into the wall-length mirror. Sounds of shattering glass echoed around the room as the reflective shards rained down around her, peppering her exposed skin with slices and cuts.

The axe tumbled from her hand and Danny leapt forward to kick it out of her reach.

"Give it up, Nia." Danny approached her slowly, dread growing in his chest. Her blood didn't smell of rage, or even fear, she smelled like anticipation. "Unlike you, I don't enjoy hurting people."

Nia limped towards the fireplace, a red trail of blood following her. "That's why you'll always lose." Nia pressed a panel along the side of the mantel. Gears clicked and the panel, only about a foot wide with a dark hole in the center, slowly slid into the wall.

What now? He braced himself for something terrible: spikes or flames, maybe even grenade blasts. Danny dove behind the long, white couch, flipping it over him for maximum cover.

Silence.

He peered around the edge of the couch.

Nia was gone, her clothes and jewelry pooled in a pile where she'd been standing.

"Nia?"

Something on the floor hissed and Danny jumped back. A *cobra* lay coiled in Nia's rumpled laundry.

"You slippery sonofabitch! You're a snake shifter?" Danny pulled out his machete and approached cautiously. "You know, machetes were pretty much *designed* for killing snakes."

"Danny!" Robin ran into the room, disheveled but grinning. She held a plastic container of glittering, rainbow-colored worms writhing inside. "I found--" she started to say, but stopped when Nia the snake hissed and swung her diamond-backed head in her direction. "What the fuck?" Robin cried.

"Watch out! It's Nia! She was a shifter before she was a vampire." Danny approached slowly. Just because she was smaller didn't mean she had lost any of her strength or speed.

Nia slithered toward the dark hole in the panel she'd opened and Danny lunged, his machete missing by a hair. He moved to block the escape hatch, seeing only death in her tiny, black gaze.

Out of the corner of his eye, he saw Robin tear the lid off of the container and spring to the window, holding the open box aloft.

Nia slithered toward him, her head waving back and forth. "Little prince, do you really think you can stop me?" Nia's voice took on a rasping whisper out of her snake's throat. "*Hortari* is part of who we are, and it's good business."

Danny darted forward again but she dodged, laughing, a terrible cackle. Distantly, Danny thought he heard a familiar screeching sound approaching. Robin caught his eye, mouthing,

"Keep her busy."

"Business, huh?" Danny taunted the snake. "You're creating slaves."

The rumbling was getting closer.

Nina chuckled. "We *all* create slaves. I just have the balls to command them."

The screech of birdcalls filled the room, and the walls shook. Robin hurled the container at Nia, showering the snake with worms, and screamed.

"Get back!"

Glass exploded behind them as the windows shattered. Dark shapes crowded and pushed each other to get inside.

Danny dove back behind the couch, pulling Robin with him. The frames of the windows groaned and half the wall broke inward.

Danny pulled Robin closer as sharp, pecking sounds filled the palatial suite.

Robin leaned closer against him. "I found them in the kitchen, some ingredient for a spell Nia was cooking." She touched his face. "I was so worried when I heard all the crashing."

Danny risked a peek over the edge of the couch. The remains of snake dotted the floor in pieces while the vultrich feasted happily on the sky worms and the pieces of snake still stuck to them. The happy flaps of their wings sent showers of discarded feathers into the air.

"Your birds took care of Nia for us." She rested her head on his shoulder.

"I guess they're good at protecting me too."

~

ROBIN LOVED the feeling of the cold window's glass against her forehead as she looked out at the vultrich chirping and pecking in their new, protected habitat. The gardens of the Blood Oasis had been the perfect biome for a vultrich nesting sanctuary. It was only the first of many that Robin had planned now that she and Danny were the new managers of the club, but she had time. Eternity, in fact.

After the giant birds killed Nia for them, a few of Nia's conscripted vamps had joined Robin on her mission to save the vultriches. Seyah in particular was rabid about opposing construction projects and utility plants which threatened to harm the vultrich's habitat.

Danny fell onto the padded bench beside the window, breathing heavy after his last hour out on the dance floor. After they'd taken down Nia, Danny had called Christopher to stand down his troops. Christopher had come anyway to ensure that his sireling and the others were okay. Christopher had been everything Robin thought a king should be: considerate, commanding, and kind. He also immediately said he would fund Robin's initiative to transport the vultrich nestlings to their new habitat.

"Any word from Samantha about the protection spell?" Danny asked. He hummed a little along with the music.

"It should be up any second now." Robin kissed his cheek. Since the grand reopening, they'd been experimenting with spells to protect their staff and clientele. Robin was overjoyed that her college roommate, Samantha, had gamely agreed to be their new head of magical security to finish working out the bugs.

Robin smiled as a flash of magic surged past her and into the fabric of the building itself. The dancers on the floor all cheered, grinding deeper into their partners.

"Want to test it out?" Danny asked.

Robin shook her head. "No need, I think we're about to see a live demonstration." She nodded toward Kendry at the bar, who was telling a stubby satyr she would not be joining him upstairs. The lovely vampire was one of the few who had decided to stay on as paid staff since she enjoyed most of the work and loved to dance. But a few of her former clients she'd been forced to entertain under the old management couldn't quite seem to understand that she was now able to say "no". The satyr started to make a grab for her, but she pushed him away. He teetered back on his hooves, and then...disappeared.

Robin swiveled to peer out the window, the satisfaction of success like a warm glow suffusing her skin. The misogynist was out past the front gates, jumping up and down and yelling. He banged against the opening of the driveway, but his fists struck against the invisible barrier, which would keep him out until Kendry decided to allow him in. Samantha's spell worked wonders at getting rid of those who weren't respectful of the rules.

"The new security system works perfectly, folks," Robin said into the walkie-talkie at her hip. She leaned forward to brush her lips against Danny's. "We did it!"

"Hmm, yes we did. I never doubted it." He tasted like bourbon and blood. She licked along the inside of his lip and his breath hitched, his hands pulling her closer until she straddled him on the bench.

"Tiger shifter blood?" She kissed him deeper, her tongue plunging to lick the inside of his cheeks and stroke along his tongue. "Yum. A horny one at that." The taste of the tiger on his lips fed her arousal, the notes of sexual urgency churning in her from even the smallest droplet from his mouth. "My favorite."

Danny's hands massaged her ass, his lips kissing her neck with enough pressure to make her gasp. Her nipples peaked and her hips swayed to the rhythm of the dance floor's music, grinding against him as her heartbeat raced.

"Do you know what's my favorite?" he purred into her mouth.

Her fingers wound into his hair, pulling him closer until his scent surrounded her. "Do you really want me to guess?"

His erect cock was flush with the top of her thighs and she rubbed her clit through her pants along his shaft, loving the friction.

Danny ran his tongue up the side of her neck. "I really don't."

She chuckled and kissed him deeply, pulling down the neck of his shirt to caress the top of his chest. "Then, my sweet, sexy love, what is your favorite?"

"Come see." He grabbed her hand and ran with her through the door, not stopping until they were outside among the trees.

Danny gathered her against his side so they were both leaning against the trunk of an oak tree. The night smelled sweet, the honeysuckle and roses from the garden overlaying the lusher smells of earth, moss, and leaves. Robin relaxed against the bark, the first time she'd taken Danny to see the vultrich nests as well as all those weekends with her parents all layering on top of one another.

"So, are you going to tell me your favorite?" she asked, turning to him. The moonlight hit his face in harsh relief, making his eyes almost glow with luminance and his skin even more smooth and kissable. She'd been so distracted: by the vultriches, by taking down Nia, with setting up the new safe space for the birds and the freed vampires to really think about how perfect her lover was. Danny was more than she'd ever dreamed was possible: funny, loyal, fun, and curious. He ran a finger down the side of her cheek and she bit her lip. He was also pants-wettingly hot.

Danny chuckled. "Well, when I dragged you out here, I had this whole speech planned. I was going to tell you that my favorite thing is you, and that you've brought me more joy in these last months together than in the hundreds of years I lived previously."

His finger caressed from her chin down along her neck to play with the edge of her button-down shirt, teasing her collarbone right inside the fabric. "And I was going to tell you that everything about you is amazing, from your protectiveness, to your daring, to your bravery, to the way your mouth wrinkles when you're annoyed with me and want me to get to the point."

Robin laughed, relaxing her mouth from where she'd been biting the inside of her cheek. Excitement bubbled in the pit of her stomach.

"And I had this whole thing where I was going to talk about everything you told me about your parents, and how nature never seemed to hold any interest to me until you showed me how to look at everything in here with love. And that love for the world is something that I never quite grasped, for all my wandering, until I met you."

He got down on one knee and Robin felt tears form in her eyes.

"Wherever you are is my home, whether it is here or centuries from now when we want to see how much the world has changed."

She hiccupped, happy sobs building in her chest. "So, you were going to say all that, huh?"

He smiled. "Yeah, but then I thought the better of it." He laughed, pulling a ring from his pocket, the rock inside the classic, gold band: black with veins of green like a vultrich's wing. "I love you more than anything else in this world, and I want to spend every day at your side."

"Yes!" Robin cried, so loud the vultrich down below in the valley called out in response, squawking and running as they tried to find the source of the sound.

"And now we run," Robin said, grabbing his hand.

"Always."

And she smiled as they sprinted back to the house. She knew she'd be running hand in hand with him forever.

Want to know more about Danny's past sireling? Check out what happens to the man he turned in the next installment of Royal Blood: The Vampire's Escape.

Dear Reader,

We hoped you enjoyed **The Vampire's Lair.** We really love this world and creating more places and people to inhabit it. Many readers wrote asking; "What's up with Lola?" Well, stay tuned for more of Lola's mysterious meddling because the adventures at AUDREY'S (and the paranormal romantic interludes) aren't over.

When we first published this series, we got a lot of emails from fans thanking us for these books. Some liked certain series and sets of characters more than others. As authors, we love feedback. Your appreciation for this world is the reason why we keep writing books in this world.

Reviews are increasingly tough to come by these days. You, the reader, have the power now to make or break a book. So, tell us what you like, what you loved, even what you hated. We'd love to hear from you.

Thank you so much for reading **The Vampire's Lair** and for spending time with our wacky brains.

Have fun, everybody

Annie & Jess ("AJ") Tipton

MEET AJ TIPTON

AJ Tipton is the pseudonym of a writing team: Annie and Jess (Get it? "AJ." You get it). Corporate drones by day, we spend our evenings writing fantasies to astound, arouse, and amuse. Located in Brooklyn, we are total dorks and love it.

Want more stories of the bizarre and wondrous? Sign up for the new publications subscription list and you'll be the first to know when new books become available. There might also be other surprises along the way. Or just contact us directly at a.j.tipton.author@gmail.com

Our ideas for future books--everything from sex robots to ghost brothels--will keep us busy for many years to come, so follow along for the fun and let us know what series you like best. We love to hear from readers.

ajtiptonauthor.wordpress.com
ajtiptonauthor@gmail.com

Made in United States
Orlando, FL
27 September 2024